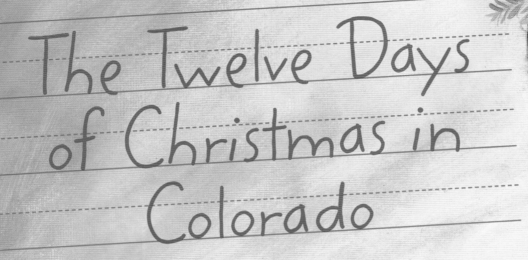

The Twelve Days of Christmas in Colorado

written by
Linda Ashman

illustrated by
Dawn Beacon

STERLING CHILDREN'S BOOKS
New York

Dear Sophie,

Are you packed yet? Just a few more days and you'll be here in Colorado, spending the Christmas holidays with us. I can't wait!

You're going to love it here. We've got bustling cities, sprawling ranches, ancient ruins, great train rides, ghost towns, and even giant sand dunes. Oh, and lots of mountains—<u>big</u> ones: more than 50 are higher than 14,000 feet! I can't wait to show you my favorite places and introduce you to some very interesting animals—including the prehistoric kind.

Now, about that packing. Be sure to bring plenty of layers. It's going to be cold and snowy in the mountains, but the plains could be much warmer. And don't forget your sunscreen. Colorado gets lots of sunshine. See you soon!

Your favorite cousin,

Zach

P.S. Hope you like surprises!

Dear Mom and Dad,

Zach wasn't kidding about surprises! He was waiting for me at the Denver airport with a big one: my very own Colorado blue spruce, the state tree. It's small now, but it will grow to be really tall—maybe more than 70 feet!

He also gave me a lark bunting named Elbert (after Mt. Elbert, Colorado's highest mountain peak). I'm going to call him Bertie. Lark buntings are Colorado's state bird. Normally they fly south for the winter, but Bertie is no ordinary bird. Zach says he's a bit emotional and bursts into song when he gets really excited.

After we left the airport—which looks like a bunch of snowy mountains— Aunt Lucy and Uncle Charlie took us to downtown Denver, Colorado's capital city. Every year they have a huge holiday lights display. Larimer Square— Denver's oldest block—was all lit up, along with lots of other buildings. When the snow started falling, Bertie couldn't contain himself and started singing "White Christmas." Now I see what Zach means. But no wonder Bertie was excited. It's beautiful here!

Love,
Snowy Sophie

P.S. Did you know Denver is called the Mile High City? That's because it's 5,280 feet above sea level!

Dear Mom and Dad,

Today we walked for miles through jungles and forests and faced a pack of wild animals. Well, sort of. Actually, we visited the Denver Zoo. First we went to see Colorado's state animal: the Rocky Mountain Bighorn Sheep. Zach says they're really well suited to the mountains because they're expert climbers. Even with those big, heavy horns, they can jump over crevices as wide as 7 feet—which comes in handy when there are mountain lions around! We saw all sorts of other animals, too—slithery snakes, noisy monkeys, brilliant birds, giraffes, cheetahs, kangaroos, elephants—you name it. And of course, my favorite: polar bears!

Speaking of bears, did you know there's a giant blue one peeking into the Colorado Convention Center? Oh, and a life-size horse on a huge red chair in front of the Central Library, a colossal cow and calf near the Denver Art Museum, and two enormous dancers near the Performing Arts Complex! Not real ones, of course, but sculptures. Aunt Lucy says Denver is very big on public art. BIG is right!

Your not-so-big daughter,
Sophie

me!

All aboard!

Zach says Colorado is a great state for train buffs. (He should know—he's one of them!) There are historic trains that chug past amazing scenery all over the state. Today we went to Colorado Springs to ride Zach's favorite—the cog railway to the top of Pikes Peak. What a view! We saw frozen lakes, and plains that stretched all the way to Kansas. No wonder Katharine Lee Bates was inspired to write "America the Beautiful" when she visited way back in 1893. Bertie was inspired to sing it, too (a bit too loudly). Pikes Peak is named after Zebulon Pike, an explorer who tried to climb it in 1806. Although it's not the tallest peak, it's high—VERY high. Between the altitude and the view, I had to catch my breath!

Afterward, we hiked through the Garden of the Gods, a park with incredible red sandstone formations. I especially liked the Kissing Camels, the Three Graces, and Balanced Rock—which Bertie thought was a perfect place to perch. The park is very popular with rock climbers. We watched them climb higher and higher till they were no more than tiny specks. Wow!

Breathlessly yours,
Sophie

Balanced Rock! →

P.S. Did you know that the Santa Tracker is based in Colorado Springs? Every year, millions of people around the world check the website of NORAD (that's the North American Aerospace Defense Command) on Christmas Eve to follow Santa's travels.

On the third day of Christmas,
my cousin gave to me . . .

3 rail cars

2 leaping sheep,
and a bunting in a spruce tree.

Dear Mom and Dad,

Even though Colorado is nowhere near the ocean, it has the tallest sand dunes in North America. The highest one is 750 feet—that would fill a LOT of sandboxes! I got to see them for myself when we visited the Great Sand Dunes National Park today. The park ranger told us how the dunes were created by all kinds of forces: movements in the earth, volcanic activity, erosion, water, and wind. It was really interesting, but climbing the dunes was even better—and rolling back down was the most fun of all!

We also saw a herd of elk grazing nearby. The male elk, or bulls, are really big. They can weigh more than 700 pounds! Zach told me elk lose their antlers every spring and grow a new set. Their winter coat has two layers and is five times warmer than their summer coat. That's important in a place where temperatures can drop far below zero. Brrrrr!

With love,
Sandy Sophie

P.S. Speaking of dressing for the season, you don't want to wear sandals here in summer. The sand can get hotter than 140 degrees—hot enough to scorch your feet!

On the fourth day of Christmas,
my cousin gave to me . . .

4 grazing elk

3 rail cars, 2 leaping sheep,
and a bunting in a spruce tree.

Hi, Mom and Dad.

When gold and silver were discovered here in 1859, mining towns sprang up all over Colorado. Today we visited Leadville, one of the most famous. The whole town is a National Historic District, with plenty of signs of its mining past. At the National Mining Hall of Fame and Museum, we saw a replica of an underground mine, old tools, a model railroad (Zach loved that), and real gold nuggets—some big ones! We also walked by the Tabor Opera House, built by Horace Tabor, one of the men who made—and then lost—a fortune here. Many famous people performed onstage, including magician and escape artist Harry Houdini and composer John Philip Sousa. When Bertie heard that, he started whistling "Stars and Stripes Forever" (apparently, he loves marching music).

Life was really hard for miners. Many gave up, and others moved on when the gold or silver ran out. When that happened, lots of busy mining camps became ghost towns—Uncle Charlie says there are hundreds of them here in the mountains. That means there must be ghosts, too. In fact, I think we saw one today!

With giant nuggets of love,
Sophie

P.S. Zach says there are other reminders of Colorado's gold rush, like the gold-plated dome of the State Capitol building, and the United States Mint in Denver, which started out as an office for weighing gold. But his favorite is found on the basketball court—the Denver Nuggets!

Hi, Mom and Dad.

Guess what? We've been practicing for the annual snow sculpture competition held here in Breckenridge in late January. Teams come from all over the world to compete, each one starting with a 12-foot-tall block of snow that weighs 20 tons—that's a lot of snowmen! The teams have several days to carve the snow into sculptures using only hand tools—things like shovels, saws, and screwdrivers. Zach says the sculptures are amazing—giant people, elephants, frogs—anything goes! We learned how to make some smaller creations of our own by packing snow into large trash bins and then flipping them over. I made a polar bear and Zach made a caboose. We're going to keep practicing so we can have our own team some day.

All that hard work made us tired—and hungry. So we piled into a horse-drawn sleigh and took a ride through a snowy meadow—with hot cocoa and cookies, of course. It was really beautiful and quiet—that is, till Bertie got excited and started belting out "Jingle Bells." Can you blame him?

Your daughter, the sculptor,
Sophie

On the sixth day of Christmas, my cousin gave to me . . .

6 frozen giants

5 golden nuggets, 4 grazing elk, 3 rail cars, 2 leaping sheep, and a bunting in a spruce tree.

Dear Mom and Dad,

How about some cave popcorn and moonmilk? No, they're not strange snack foods, they're <u>speleothems</u>, a fancy word for cave formations. Today we toured some amazing caverns in Glenwood Springs. We saw pointy stalactites and stalagmites, twisty helictites, and beautiful gypsum flowers—curvy speleothems that aren't really flowers at all. One formation looked like a huge wedding cake, and others like enormous chess pieces. It made me wonder if giants once lived there.

We didn't meet any giants, but we did see some other residents: bats! Bertie discovered them hibernating while he was flying around. Aunt Lucy said that bats do very important work by eating insects, pollinating plants, and spreading seeds, so we were careful not to disturb them—they need their sleep!

This town is also famous for its hot springs pool—the largest one in the world. It's two blocks long and holds more than a million gallons of water! After all that walking, we were happy to soak in it. And with the moon shining, and the snow falling, it was magical.

Love,
Sophie the Spelunker
(a fancy word for cave explorer)

P.S. How can you tell the difference between a stalactite and a stalagmite? Stalac<u>t</u>ites hold TIGHT to the ceiling and stalag<u>m</u>ites MIGHT reach the ceiling.

Dear Mom and Dad,

If you lived in Colorado 150 million years ago, you would have had some BIG neighbors—dinosaurs! You can find dinosaur remains all over the state, in places like Dinosaur Ridge, Dinosaur National Monument, and Picketwire Canyonlands Dinosaur Tracksite—which has more than 1,300 dino footprints!

Today we visited Dinosaur Journey Museum near Grand Junction. We saw bones, skeletons, fossils, and robotic replicas of all sorts of dinosaurs, including the scary, meat-eating Allosaurus, the crested Dilophosaurus, and the bony-plated Stegosaurus—which also happens to be the state fossil.

Bertie was especially interested in the Velociraptor. Although they couldn't fly, scientists believe Velociraptors had feathers and were closely related to modern birds. (Bertie said he did see a resemblance to his Great Uncle Fred.)

We also visited a nearby trail loaded with bones and fossils, and saw a quarry that was probably a dinosaur watering hole at one time. Imagine having to share your water with an Allosaurus. Yikes! I can't wait to come back when it's warmer and join an actual dinosaur dig.

Your future paleontologist (that's someone who studies fossils), Sophie

Uncle Fred?

On the eighth day of Christmas,
my cousin gave to me . . .

8 dinos roaming

7 bats a-napping, **6** frozen giants,
5 golden nuggets, **4** grazing elk,
3 rail cars, **2** leaping sheep,
and a bunting in a spruce tree.

Greetings from your new Junior Ranger! Today Zach and I earned our badges at Mesa Verde, something you can do at many national parks. We learned about the Ancestral Puebloan people who settled here about 1,400 years ago. Although they had different kinds of homes, they're most famous for their cliff dwellings—sort of like big apartment buildings carved into the sides of cliffs. We toured Spruce Tree House, one of the largest. It had about 130 rooms and 8 kivas (those were important underground rooms where they had special ceremonies).

We also learned about their expert basket-making skills. The baskets were very important for carrying seeds, corn, piñon nuts—even water. They cooked in them, too. We tried making our own, but it wasn't easy, especially when Bertie kept plucking at my supplies. I'm sorry to say I won't be bringing home a beautiful basket—but I do have a silly new hat—and Bertie has a cozy new nest!

The Ancestral Puebloans mysteriously disappeared from Mesa Verde about 700 years ago. For a long time, people thought they'd vanished. But archeologists figured out that they'd actually moved to what's now Arizona and New Mexico, where their descendants still live.

Love,
Ranger Sophie

P.S. Here's a riddle for you: Today I was in four places at one time. Where was I?
(Answer: Four Corners Monument, where the borders of Utah, Colorado, Arizona, and New Mexico all meet!)

On the ninth day of Christmas,
my cousin gave to me . . .

9 woven baskets

8 dinos roaming, 7 bats a-napping, 6 frozen giants,
5 golden nuggets, 4 grazing elk, 3 rail cars, 2 leaping sheep,
and a bunting in a spruce tree.

Dear Mom and Dad,

Imagine this: you're traveling across the prairie in a creaky covered wagon. You're hungry and cold, and the wind is blowing snow across the trail. Your food is nearly gone, you're worried about blizzards, and you wonder if your wagon—and the oxen pulling it—will survive the trip. After two months of hard travel, you see a building in the distance. At last—it's Bent's Old Fort!

Today we visited a replica of the fort, an important trading post along the Santa Fe Trail—the main road that connected Missouri to what is now Santa Fe, New Mexico. Back in the 1830s and '40s, many people stopped here to make trades, stock up on supplies, get their wagons fixed, and eat a good meal. We explored the kitchen, living areas, blacksmith shop, and the trade room—which was like a big general store. Trappers, traders, soldiers, Native Americans, and others exchanged all kinds of things at the fort—buffalo pelts, kettles, fabric, beads, knives, and seashells, plus treats like sugar and chocolate.

Travel was really rough back then. A wagon trip from Missouri to New Mexico could take nearly three months. In a car, it would take less than a day!

Love,
Trader Sophie

P.S. At the fort we saw oxen, colorful Dominique chickens, and Spanish Barb horses—a favorite of Spanish and Mexican cowboys. Bertie especially liked the peacocks!

On the tenth day of Christmas, my cousin gave to me . . .

10 covered wagons

9 woven baskets,
8 dinos roaming, **7** bats a-napping,
6 frozen giants, **5** golden nuggets,
4 grazing elk, **3** rail cars, **2** leaping sheep,
and a bunting in a spruce tree.

Dear Mom and Dad,

Giddy-up! Today we went to Uncle Charlie and Aunt Lucy's ranch on the eastern plains near Burlington. Their house is like a museum, packed with Old West furniture, posters, books—even clothes! We dressed up in cowboy duds, then Aunt Lucy saddled up Ike and Mamie so Zach could teach me to ride. We're practicing for the rodeo at the National Western Stock Show, held in Denver every January for more than 100 years. They have lots of contests, like bronc riding, barrel racing, and team roping, plus all sorts of great performers. My favorite is the horse dancing. Mamie's a little old for dancing, but I loved riding her anyway.

We passed a buffalo ranch on the way here. Uncle Charlie told us there used to be millions of buffalo on the Great Plains, but they were hunted so much they almost became extinct. Luckily, people pushed hard to preserve them, so they've survived. I was happy to hear that. Bertie was, too. So happy, in fact, he started singing "Home on the Range."

Your cowgirl,
Sophie

On the eleventh day of Christmas, my cousin gave to me . . .

11 horses prancing

10 covered wagons, **9** woven baskets, **8** dinos roaming,
7 bats a-napping, **6** frozen giants, **5** golden nuggets,
4 grazing elk, **3** rail cars, **2** leaping sheep,
and a bunting in a spruce tree.

Dear Mom and Dad,

For my last day here we drove to the mountains to hit the powder bright and early. I slalomed through the bumpy moguls on a really steep run. I was racing so fast, I felt like an Olympic skier!

Well, actually, I was only on the bunny slope. And I wasn't going all that fast—mostly, I was trying not to fall!—but it was so much fun. Between Zach's instructions and my ski lesson, I learned a lot. Now I know about equipment, how to get on a chair lift, how to turn, and—most important of all—how to stop!

While I had my lesson, Zach was shredding in the terrain park, doing jumps and riding the rails. Basically, that means he was doing tricks on his snowboard. He's a pretty good skier and snowboarder, but can't wait to try the Black Diamond trails—those are the hardest runs.

Colorado has tons of winter activities, but Zach says it's beautiful in the summertime, too, when you can go hiking, biking, rafting, and horseback riding. Hmmmm, what are we doing for summer vacation this year? I know just the place to go!

Love,
Super Skier Sophie,
missing Colorado already

On the twelfth day of Christmas,
my cousin gave to me . . .

12 skiers swooshing

11 horses prancing, **10** covered wagons, **9** woven baskets,
8 dinos roaming, **7** bats a-napping, **6** frozen giants,
5 golden nuggets, **4** grazing elk, **3** rail cars,
2 leaping sheep, and a bunting in a spruce tree.

DENVER BOTANIC GARDENS
THE CENTENNIAL STATE
Average Temperature
January: 24°F
July: 68°F
Telluride Film Festival
Isaac Slade
Musician/Songwriter
Lead Singer of
THE FRAY
Durango & Silverton
Narrow Gauge
Railroad & Museum
DENVER MARCH
POWWOW
Chief Ouray
1833-1880
Leader of the
Ute Indian Tribe
GO NUGGETS!
DENVER
GO ROCKIES!
UNITED STATES AIR FORCE ACADEMY
Roy Halladay
Pitcher and
Cy Young
Award Winner
Lindsey Vonn
OLYMPIC GOLD
MEDALIST
Palisade
Peach Festival
S.E. DENVER
13
BASEBALL
LOVELAND
The Sweetheart City
Re-mailing Valentines
Since 1946
SKI COLORADO
HAMILTON
HUSKIES
Rock!
Visit
Rocky Mountain
National Park

Colorado: The Centennial State

Capital: Denver • **State abbreviation:** CO • **Largest city:** Denver • **State bird:** lark bunting • **State flower:** Rocky Mountain columbine • **State tree:** Colorado blue spruce • **State Insect:** Colorado hairstreak butterfly • **State fossil:** stegosaurus • **State animal:** Rocky Mountain bighorn sheep • **State reptile:** western painted turtle • **State motto:** "Nil Sine Numine" ("Nothing without the Deity" or "Nothing without Providence") • **State songs:** "Where the Columbines Grow," by A. J. Fynn, and "Rocky Mountain High," by John Denver

Some Famous Coloradans:

Margaret Tobin Brown (1867–1932) moved to Leadville in her late teens and married a miner, "J.J." Brown, soon after. Despite humble beginnings, they made a fortune in gold mining and bought a mansion in Denver, now called the Molly Brown House Museum. A prominent socialite, activist, philanthropist, and suffragette, "Maggie" became famous as "The Unsinkable Molly Brown" after surviving the *Titanic* disaster.

M. Scott Carpenter (1925–) grew up in Boulder and attended the University of Colorado. As one of the "Mercury Seven," he was a pioneer in human space flight. He also participated in the Navy's SEALAB II project, earning the title of Aquanaut as well as Astronaut.

Mary Coyle Chase (1907–1981) was born and raised in Denver. The author of many articles, plays, and children's books, she was most famous for writing the play "Harvey," which won the Pulitzer Prize for drama, and was made into a successful movie in 1950.

William Harrison "Jack" Dempsey (1895–1983), born in Manassa, was a famous boxer and, later, an actor and restaurant owner. He reigned as World Heavyweight Boxing Champion from 1919 to 1926.

Cleo Parker Robinson (c.1948–), a Denver native, is a prominent dancer, choreographer, teacher, and activist. She founded and directs Cleo Parker Robinson Dance, an award-winning dance ensemble that performs all over the world.

Byron White (1917–2002) was born in Fort Collins, and graduated from the University of Colorado. He was valedictorian of his class and an All-American football player. In 1962, President John F. Kennedy named him to the U.S. Supreme Court; he served until his retirement in 1993.

To Jack and Jackson, my favorite Colorado companions.
—L.A.

To my wonderful parents, Bruce and Judy, who encouraged me to keep painting.
—D.B.

ACKNOWLEDGMENTS

Many thanks to all the friendly, knowledgeable, and informative people at national parks, historic sites, museums, and other attractions throughout Colorado who patiently answered my many questions. Extra special thanks to Meredith Mundy, born and raised in Colorado, for her thoughtful suggestions and excellent editorial advice, and to Isabel Stein and Andrea Santoro for their keen eyes and fact-checking expertise. I'm also grateful to the Denver Public Library system—an invaluable resource and one of the city's true gems—and, especially, to the always-helpful staff at the Cherry Creek branch, my second home.
—L.A.

Distributed in Canada by Sterling Publishing
c/o Canadian Manda Group, 165 Dufferin Street
Toronto, Ontario, Canada M6K 3H6
Distributed in the United Kingdom by GMC Distribution Services
Castle Place, 166 High Street, Lewes, East Sussex, England BN7 1XU
Distributed in Australia by Capricorn Link (Australia) Pty. Ltd.
P.O. Box 704, Windsor, NSW 2756, Australia

The artwork in this book was created using acrylic paints.

For information about custom editions, special sales, and premium and corporate purchases, please contact Sterling Special Sales at 800-805-5489 or specialsales@sterlingpublishing.com.

Printed in China
Lot #:
4 6 8 10 9 7 5
07/15

www.sterlingpublishing.com/kids

CANADA

Washington

Montana

Oregon

Idaho

Wyoming

Nevada

Utah

Colorado

California

Arizona

New Mexico

Alaska

Hawaii

(NOT TO SCALE)

MEXICO